WALT DISNEY'S
Pooh Sleepytime Stories

gb **GOLDEN PRESS • NEW YORK**
WESTERN PUBLISHING COMPANY, INC.
RACINE, WISCONSIN

Contents

Winnie-the-Pooh Opens the Door

It was eight o'clock in the evening—one of
Winnie-the-Pooh's very favorite times. "Next
to breakfast-time and lunchtime and teatime,"
said Pooh, "I like eight o'clock best. That's when
I put on my nightshirt and my nightcap and get
into bed. It's when I go to sleep and dream.
Tonight I may dream about honey."

Pooh put on his nightshirt and his cap. He got
into bed and closed his eyes. But before he could
go to sleep and dream about anything, there was
a brisk tap-tapping at the door.

Pooh sighed. "Now who is calling at this
hour?" said he. Since there was only one way to
find out, he got out of bed and opened the door.

Gopher stood on the doorstep. There was a
hole in the path behind him. Gopher had
tunneled his way to Pooh's house.

"I hope I didn't wake you," said Gopher. Then, without waiting for Pooh to answer, Gopher stepped to one side. Three very young gophers scrambled out of the hole in the path.

"My nephews!" said Gopher. "They want to see how bears live. Pooh bears, that is."

Pooh was pleased that the gophers wanted to see his home, and he invited them in. They admired his chairs and table. They listened to the clock ticktock on the wall. Then they peeped into his cupboard. There on the shelf stood three pots of honey. Christopher Robin had given them to Pooh only that afternoon.

"What's in the pots?" asked one young gopher.

"Is it something to eat?" said the second.

"May we taste it?" said the third.

"Certainly," said Pooh, who firmly believed that gophers did not care for honey.

Pooh got three saucers and spooned three small dollops of honey into them. He gave the saucers to the young gophers. And before you could say, "Hundred Acre Wood," the gophers had eaten all the honey and were asking for more.

"But gophers don't like honey!" cried Pooh.

"These gophers do," said Gopher.

Pooh gave them a bit more, then a bit more, and then again a bit more. All the honey in the first honey pot was gone.

The young gophers thanked Pooh. They trotted out and disappeared into the hole in the path. Gopher followed them.

"My!" said Pooh. "A whole pot of honey gone! At least I have two pots left. Now I can snuggle down in bed and..."

There came a thundering knock at the door.

"Now what?" moaned Pooh, and he opened the door.

"Pooh bear, thank goodness you're home!" said Rabbit. He looked frightfully upset. "An awful thing happened. Dampness in my root cellar! My carrots are all mildewed!"

"Oh," said Pooh. "That's too bad."

Pooh didn't think that carrots were truly important, but he hated to see Rabbit upset.

"I don't suppose you have any carrots?" said Rabbit.

Pooh did not.

"Oh, my!" said Rabbit. "Seventeen of my youngest relations are coming tonight for carrot cake. I can't send them away hungry. Are you sure you don't have any carrots?"

Pooh was sure.

"Or anything?" said Rabbit. He gave Pooh a stern glance. It was the sort of glance that makes a bear go to his cupboard. Of course when Pooh opened the cupboard, there were two jars of honey on the shelf. Rabbit was quite pleased to take one of them. "Honey isn't what small rabbits like best," said he, "but it will have to do for tonight."

"I am going to bed," said Pooh, after Rabbit left. "I will not open my door again tonight. Instead I will pull the covers up to my nose, and I'll close my eyes and think of the bumbly sound bees make when they fly through fields of clover and..."

At that, there was a gentle rapping at the door. "Pooh dear, are you there?" called Kanga.

Pooh groaned. He couldn't pretend he wasn't there. Not to Kanga. So he opened the door and let Kanga in. Roo hopped in after her.

"I want to bake a cake for Roo's breakfast," said Kanga, "and would you believe that I don't have a bit of honey to sweeten it?"

"Yes," said Pooh sadly, "I'd believe that."

So I wondered..." Kanga went on.

Of course," said Pooh. He said it quickly, for Roo had jumped onto the bed and begun to bounce.

Pooh gave his last jar of honey to Kanga, and Kanga went off through the forest with Roo. Pooh began to smooth his bed where Roo had jumped on it.

Then there came another knock at the door.

"No!" cried Pooh. "Go away! I want to go to bed. And I don't have any more honey!"

"You don't?" Christopher Robin came in. "What happened to the three jars I gave you this afternoon?" he asked.

"Oh, Christopher Robin! It's you!" cried Pooh.

Pooh told Christopher Robin about the gophers. He told him about Rabbit and his relations and Kanga and her cake.

"What a kind bear you are, Pooh," said Christopher Robin. "But now you had better go to bed. You look quite sleepy after being up so late with your friends."

Pooh did go to bed. He lay warm under the covers while Christopher Robin read him a story. It was a story about a circus, and Christopher Robin read it in a quiet, gentle voice. Soon Pooh was sound asleep and dreaming.

He dreamed that he was at a circus. In fact, he dreamed that he was the dancing bear *in* the circus, which is quite a different thing and ever so much more important. Everyone who saw him clapped and shouted, "Bravo!" They crowded around and gave him pots and pots of honey.

14

15

When Pooh woke up it was morning.
Christopher Robin was gone, but Gopher was
in the room. So was Kanga. And so was Rabbit.

"I tunneled my way into a bee tree," said
Gopher, "so I brought you a present."

He put three jars of honey on Pooh's table.

"My young relations got into my pantry and
found these," said Rabbit. "I didn't even know I
had them."

He put two jars of honey on Pooh's table.

"Roo's cake turned out so well," said Kanga,
"that I baked another one especially for you."

She put the cake on the table—and a very nice
cake it was, all glistening with honey. It was just
the sort of cake bears like. Pooh bears, that is.

From that day on, Pooh always opened his
door when his friends knocked. Unless he was
sound asleep, of course. Which he often was.

Are you?

Piglet Goes Exploring

Piglet sat on his doorstep. He watched the sky turn from a pink sunset sky to a deep blue evening sky. He watched the stars come out, one by one.

"I wonder," said Piglet, "what it would be like to go exploring at night."

No one answered, but the wind made soft shushing noises in the trees.

"I haven't been out much at night," said Piglet. "Perhaps it's time that I went."

And he did.

"First I'll call on Owl," said Piglet, as he trotted through the woods. "He'll say, 'Ho there, Piglet!' and 'My word, it's Piglet!' He'll tell me I'm a brave Piglet to be out exploring at night."

But when Piglet came to Owl's house, Owl didn't say, "Ho, Piglet!" He didn't say, "My word, it's Piglet!" He didn't say anything, for Owl wasn't home.

Then Piglet heard a fluttering and a rustling and a peeping high up in the tree where Owl lived.

"Is that you, Owl?" cried Piglet.

When Owl didn't answer, Piglet decided that it was probably no one at all. "And if it's no one at all," said Piglet, "it won't hurt to climb up and see."

Piglet did climb up. He saw three baby birds
sound asleep in their nest. They were warm and
safe under their mother's wings.

"Hello," said Piglet. "I'm Piglet, and I'm out
exploring."

"Well you should be at home, little Piglet,"
said the mother bird, "snug and cozy in your
bed. Now go away before you wake my
children."

Piglet climbed down from the tree and went
on. The moon was up by now, and Piglet's
shadow ran with him. It hopped when he hopped.
It stopped when he stopped. But when he spoke,
it said not a word.

"It would be nice," said Piglet, "to have
someone to talk with while I'm exploring."

Just as he said this, Piglet came to a clearing. In the middle of the clearing was someone's front door.

"That looks like Rabbit's house," said Piglet, "except that Rabbit's house is in another place entirely. I wonder who lives here."

Piglet put his head in at the door to see.

And what did he see?

He saw a fine, soft featherbed. He saw four of Rabbit's youngest relations snuggled all together in the bed, with the quilt pulled up to their noses. He saw the mother and daddy rabbit sitting by the fire.

"What are you doing, little Piglet?" said the mother rabbit.

"I'm exploring," said Piglet.

"Well don't do it here," said she. "You should be at home, snug and cozy in your bed. Now go away before you wake my children."

So Piglet went away. After a bit he stopped
and listened. Some frogs were croaking to the
moon.

"I'll go and talk with the frogs," said Piglet.
"They won't tell me to go away."

The frogs didn't tell Piglet to run away. But
when they saw him coming they stopped
croaking. They dove into their pond and hid.

"It's lonely to go exploring," said Piglet to his
shadow. He looked around at the dark woods.
"Perhaps I should be at home, snug and cozy in
my bed," he said. "But I'm not at home. And
I'm not anywhere else that I know of. And I
don't think I know where home *is!*"

No sooner had Piglet said this than a shadow
glided over his head and perched on a tree
nearby. Two great eyes stared at Piglet through
the dark.

"Hello," said Piglet. He said it in a small,
shaky voice. "I'm Piglet, and I'm out
exploring."

"Ho, Piglet!" said the shadowy creature with
the big eyes. "My word, it *is* Piglet!"

"Owl!" cried Piglet. "Oh, I'm *so* glad to see
you!"

"I should hope so," said Owl. "Now what's all this about exploring?"

"It seemed like a good idea when I started," said Piglet, "but it doesn't seem like a good idea now. I wish I were home, snug and cozy in my bed. But I'm not sure where home is. I thought it was over that way." Piglet pointed. "You don't suppose someone moved it while I wasn't looking?" he asked.

"Perhaps," said Owl. "That can happen when very small animals like Piglets go exploring at night. Never mind. We'll find it."

Owl began to fly through the forest. Piglet scampered after him. Soon they were back in Piglet's own part of the forest. They were at the place where the Six Pine Trees grow. Then Piglet saw his own house, and it was just where he had left it.

"No one moved it after all," said Piglet to Owl.

Owl flew away, and Piglet went into his house.

It was warm in Piglet's house, with the fire making little sputtery crackles and the shadows flickering in the corners. They were friendly shadows. They were the shadows Piglet knew. Piglet washed his face and brushed his teeth and got into his bed. It was snug and cozy, just as he thought it would be. He pulled the covers up around his ears and went to sleep.

And if he ever went exploring at night again, I haven't heard of it.

Have you?

Owl Finds a Home

Owl came home early one morning, which is
the way it is with owls. He found Rabbit waiting at
his house.

"I'm afraid," said Rabbit, "that something has
happened to your front door."

And indeed something had. Owl's front door
had fallen off its hinges and was lying in the
middle of Owl's parlor.

"Oh, dear!" said Owl.

"Yes," said Rabbit.

"How dreadful!" said Owl.

"Exactly," said Rabbit.

"Termites, I suppose," said Owl. "Or dry rot,
perhaps. It will spread to the rest of the house
in no time. I must find another place to live."

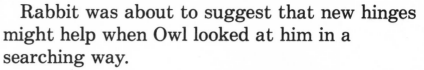

Rabbit was about to suggest that new hinges might help when Owl looked at him in a searching way.

"Surely," said Owl, "with my many friends, I'll have no trouble. I would think that you'd be *happy* to have me move in."

"Move in?" said Rabbit. "You mean with me?"

"How kind of you to suggest it," said Owl. "But let's hurry. It's seven o'clock, and I'm usually asleep by now."

"Oh, dear!" said Rabbit, but Owl seemed not to hear.

So Owl moved into Rabbit's house together with the clock that had belonged to his grandfather and the sampler which his grandmother had made which said, "East or West, Home Is Best." He brought his books, of course, and his desk and his inkstand and his chair. And when he had this great pile of things heaped up in Rabbit's underground home, there wasn't a great deal of room for Rabbit. Or for Owl. Not that Owl minded, for he hopped onto the back of his chair and went fast asleep.

And Rabbit? Why Rabbit had invited his young relations to visit, and they were delighted to see Owl's many curious possessions. They played hide-and-seek among the books and the papers, and they climbed up onto the desk and then jumped off.

Owl opened his eyes and stared at them. He sighed.

"No help for it, I suppose," he said.

So Owl packed up his things and went on through the forest to Pooh's house. There was Pooh, standing in his garden admiring his flowers. Owl told Pooh all about the termites in his house—or perhaps it was dry rot—and about Rabbit's young relations.

"One hates to hurt Rabbit's feelings," said Owl, "but I really had to move on."

"Of course," said Pooh, in a friendly fashion.

"I knew you'd agree," said Owl, and immediately he moved his things into Pooh's house.

"Thank goodness you don't have dozens of young relations who stay up all day long," said Owl as he settled himself to sleep.

Now Pooh did not have young relations, but he did have a habit of making up little poems and singing little songs to himself all day long. Owl tried not to hear the poems or listen to the songs, but he couldn't help it.

"I'll move to Kanga's house," said Owl at last. "Kanga will send Roo outdoors to play in the sunshine, and I will have peace and quiet—and sleep!"

So Owl moved again. And Kanga did send Roo outdoors. But then Kanga set to work cleaning house. She moved things and she scrubbed things and she clattered things about. She even dusted Owl's desk and washed out his inkstand.

"This will never do," said Owl. "I'll go to Piglet's house. He has no young relations and he doesn't sing much and he never dusts!"

So Owl moved on. But when Owl reached Piglet's house, Tigger was there. He was bouncing on his tail, as Tiggers do, and shouting to Piglet. "Come on!" he cried. "You can do it! It's fun!"

Owl did not even unload his things. Instead he went on to Eeyore's gloomy part of the forest. "It's sure to be quiet there," said Owl, "and I can sleep."

Indeed it was quiet. But Owl soon saw that all of his treasured possessions would never fit into Eeyore's little house. "And it's going to rain!" cried Owl. "Oh, whatever will I do?"

Christopher Robin happened to come along
just then and find Owl standing there with his
clock and his books and his desk and all the
other things. Of course Owl told him about the
termites—or the dry rot. He told him about
Rabbit's young relations, too, and how Pooh
sang and Kanga cleaned and Tigger bounced.

"And Eeyore's house is too small for me,"
wailed Owl, "and I'm so sleepy. I need a home of
my own!"

"Yes, you do," said Christopher Robin. And he
took Owl and his possessions back to Owl's own
tree. In less time than it takes to tell, he fixed
the door by putting on new hinges. "For that's
all that was wrong," he told Owl. "The hinges
had worn out."

So Owl moved back into his own dear home,
with his clock and his books and his inkstand.
Christopher Robin tiptoed away, leaving Owl to
enjoy the nicest daytime nap you can imagine.

Can you imagine such a nap?

Roo Stays Up

It was almost bedtime in the Hundred Acre Wood, and Kanga was fixing Roo's bath.

"When I grow up," said Roo, "I'll never go to bed. I'll stay up every night and do just as I please."

"Of course, Roo dear," said Kanga. She tested the water with her elbow to see if it was warm enough, which it was. "All right," she said, "in you go!"

"In a minute," said Roo.

"Not in a minute," said Kanga. "Now!"

So Roo got in. Kanga washed behind his ears. She scrubbed his back. Roo waggled his hands to make little waves in the water. Then he swished the soap around to make lots of suds. He piled the suds against the sides of the tub and pretended they were snowdrifts.

Kanga watched quietly for a long time. Then she said, "That's enough. Time to get out."

Roo kicked his feet to break up the soapsuds. "Not right now," he said.

"Now," said Kanga, and she lifted Roo out of the tub and stood him in front of the fire. She rubbed him all over with a towel until he tingled from head to toe. Then she pulled his nightshirt on over his head. "And now, into bed with you," she said, "as soon as you've brushed your teeth."

Roo did brush his teeth. He brushed up and down. He brushed back and forth. He brushed in circles.

"Enough!" cried Kanga. "To bed!"

"But where's my blanket?" asked Roo. "You know the one I mean. My very own blanket with the pink flowers on it. I can't go to sleep without my blanket. I never do!"

"Oh, dear!" said Kanga. She opened the linen cupboard, but the blanket wasn't there. It wasn't in the toy box, either, or the dresser drawers. It wasn't under any of the chairs.

"How very strange," said Kanga at last. "I can't find it. It simply isn't here. If you can't sleep without it, perhaps you *will* have to stay up all night."

"I will?" cried Roo.

"So it seems," said Kanga. "It won't hurt you. After all, you *are* quite grown-up—for a small Roo."

Kanga put on her nightgown and her nightcap. "Do try to be quiet," she said. Then she got into her own bed.

"You mean you're not going to stay up with me?" said Roo, in a surprised way.

"You don't need me, and I want to go to bed. Most grown-ups do," said Kanga. She closed her eyes, and soon Roo heard soft, regular breathing.

"She's asleep," said Roo. "*Now* I can do just as I please!" Then, oddly enough, Roo couldn't decide what might please him.

It would have been nice to hear a story, but Roo couldn't read to himself very well, and Kanga seemed to be sleeping soundly indeed.

Roo tried turning somersaults, but without Kanga to say, "Wonderful, Roo!" and "Do it again, Roo!" somersaults weren't much fun.

Roo looked into the pantry. There was bread there, but without Kanga to toast it for him and to spread it with butter and marmalade, it didn't seem worth bothering about.

Roo thought and thought. "What was it I wanted to do when I wanted to stay up all night?" he said to himself. The more he tried to remember, the more he nodded. The more he nodded the more he yawned. The more he yawned the heavier his eyes grew. At last his eyes closed altogether, and he fell asleep on the warm hearth.

When Roo woke up the room was cold and the fire was almost out.

"Perhaps I *had* better go to bed," said Roo to himself. "It's awfully nice to stay up by myself. I'll do it again soon. But right now I'm chilly, and I'll wake Kanga if I bring in more wood for the fire. Besides...besides..."

Roo stopped. He couldn't think of another good reason to go to bed. He just went. And under his coverlet he found his special blanket—the one with the pink flowers. It was exactly where he had put it while Kanga was fixing his bath. He settled down and held it against his cheek. Soon he was fast asleep.

Perhaps Kanga looked over and saw him find the blanket. Perhaps she didn't. If she did, I'll never tell.

And I'm sure neither will you.

Eeyore Goes to Sleep

The moon was up over the Hundred Acre Wood. "It's as bright as day," said Tigger, and he bounced down the path near the Six Pine Trees. "But it's much too bright for sleeping. I'll go and call on Rabbit!"

When Tigger reached Rabbit's house and knocked at the door, nothing happened for quite a long time. At last Rabbit opened the door.

"Do go away, Tigger," said Rabbit. "And don't bounce. Walk quietly. I'm trying to sleep."

Rabbit closed his door and Tigger went away as quietly as a Tigger could. He didn't bounce again until he came to Kanga's house. But then he couldn't help bouncing. Kanga was so kind. She hardly ever said things like, "Go away, Tigger," or "Don't bounce, Tigger." What Kanga usually said was, "My, that was lovely, Tigger! Bounce higher!"

But on this particular night, Kanga looked out of the window before Tigger could knock at the door. "If you're going to bounce, you can't stay," she said. "Roo is asleep, and I'll be going to bed soon."

Tigger went away, and he didn't bounce again until he reached Owl's house.

"Owl is sure to be awake," thought Tigger. "Owls are always awake at night. Perhaps Owl will come out and watch me bounce in the moonlight."

But Owl looked cross and sleepy when he answered the door. "A band of Rabbit's young relations played near my tree and kept me awake all day," said Owl. "Are you going to bounce here and keep me awake all night?"

Tigger hurried off. He hadn't any intention of behaving like Rabbit's young relations.

For a long time Tigger wandered in the woods and felt very lonely. At last he came to that gloomy place where Eeyore, the old gray donkey lived.

"I suppose I'd better not stay," thought Tigger sadly. "Eeyore is probably asleep, too."

But Eeyore wasn't asleep. Instead, he was lying half in and half out of his house. He was staring straight ahead, and he was frowning as if he had forgotten something terribly important.

"One!" said he, in a hopeful way. Then he shook his head. "It's no use," said he. "It may work for some, but I don't see any. Not that I thought I would. I tried, and I didn't."

"Didn't what, Eeyore?" asked Tigger.

"Didn't see any sheep," said Eeyore.

"Sheep?" Tigger looked around. "There aren't any sheep in these woods," he said.

"Then that explains it," said Eeyore. "Owl said that if I couldn't sleep, I should count sheep—slowly, you know, one, two, three, four. Then I'd get drowsy and nod off. But if there aren't any sheep, I can't count them."

"I suppose not," said Tigger. "What do the sheep do while you count them?"

"They jump over a fence," said Eeyore. "But they don't because there aren't any. Sheep, that is. No fence, either."

Tigger said, "Hah!" Then he took a turn around the meadow, bouncing in the moonlight. He said, "Ho!" in a loud voice and bounced back to Eeyore.

"If you can't count sheep," said he, "perhaps it would do as well for you to count Tiggers."

"Leaping over a fence?" asked Eeyore.

"We'll pretend there is a fence," said Tigger.

Eeyore sighed. "Can't be done. How can I count Tiggers when you're the only one?"

here

there

"Watch!" said Tigger. He bounced from here
to there. Then he bounced from there back to
here. He did it again—and again and again.
Eeyore began to count—one, two, three, four.

Eeyore counted. Tigger bounced. And after
Eeyore had gotten to eleventeen several times,
his eyes closed.

here

there

Tigger kept bouncing until the moon went
down and the night grew dark. Then Tigger
stopped and listened. Eeyore was breathing in a
deep, snorting, snuffly, gruffly way—exactly like
a donkey who is asleep and dreaming of
meadows filled with sweet green grass and
delicious purple thistles.

"Wonderful!" said Tigger softly. Then he
bounced home through the dark night and went
to sleep, too.

Wouldn't you?

Pooh Does a Good Deed

One stormy night, Pooh sat toasting his toes at the fire and watching the flames chase each other up the chimney. He felt just as warm and cozy as a Pooh bear can. And he was very happy until he thought of Eeyore, the old gray donkey.

"Oh, dear," said Pooh. "It's gloomy in Eeyore's part of the forest even on a nice day. What must it be like tonight with the wind blowing and the rain coming down? And Eeyore's little house is only made of sticks. Perhaps it leaks."

Once having thought of Eeyore, Pooh found that he couldn't stop. He tried getting into bed and pulling the covers over his head, but that didn't help. He went right on thinking of Eeyore.

"It's no use," said Pooh. "I can't leave Eeyore out in the cold and the wet. I'll go and invite him to spend the night with me."

Pooh put on his raincoat and his rain hat and set out. He hadn't gone far when he bumped into something or someone.

"Hallo there, Pooh," said Piglet.
"Ah, Piglet," said Pooh. "It's you."
"Wet night," said Piglet. He was carrying an umbrella. "I was just going to see how Eeyore is."
"That's funny," said Pooh. "So was I."
"In that case," said Piglet, "we can go together."

The two walked on, and soon they saw
someone hopping through the rain. In fact they
saw two someones. There was Kanga with a
shawl over her head. There was Roo, who was
having a lovely time jumping in all the puddles.

"We're going to see how Eeyore is in his poor
little hut," Kanga said. "I've brought a raincoat
to put over him, and we'll ask him to come and
spend the night."

"Just what we were going to do," said Pooh.

At that moment, Rabbit came running along the path bumping into everybody. "Oh," he said, "are all of you going to check on Eeyore, too? I'm taking him some galoshes."

There was a hooting and a swishing of wings, and Owl swooped down and landed on a tree limb near Kanga.

"The stream is rising," said Owl. "I'm going to warn Eeyore."

But before he could do it, Tigger came bouncing down the path. He had a fine big bottle of Extract of Malt.

"It's strengthening medicine for Eeyore," said Tigger. "He'll need strengthening after being out in the cold rain. And Tiggers don't need so much strengthening. Tiggers are quite strong to begin with."

Tigger bounced on.

"It's nice of Tigger to share his Extract of Malt with Eeyore," said Pooh as he walked along.

"Especially when Tigger likes it so much himself," said Piglet.

With that, they all came to the part of the forest known as Eeyore's gloomy place. On this stormy night it was terribly gloomy indeed—or it would have been were it not for Christopher Robin. He was there with a big umbrella.

"I've invited Eeyore to come and stay with me until the storm is over," said Christopher Robin.

"If it ever is," said Eeyore, "which doesn't seem likely. Not that anybody asked me, you understand. But then, they hardly ever do."

"I'd be very happy if you would *all* stay with me until the storm is over," said Christopher Robin.

So back they went, trooping through the forest, until they came to Christopher Robin's house.

They had a lovely tea then, and they all curled up in front of the fire. Owl perched on the mantel and Piglet wrapped himself in the hearth rug. Pooh settled down in a nice big chair. Then they all slept soundly, listening to the rain on the roof. And although the storm lasted for some time, no one complained a bit.

I wouldn't complain. Would you?

45